Fragments of Perseus
Michael McClure

ALSO BY MICHAEL MCCLURE

Poetry
Hymns to Saint Geryon
Dark Brown
The New Book/A Book of Torture
Ghost Tantras
Star
September Blackberries
Rare Angel
Jaguar Skies
Antechamber

Essays
Meat Science Essays
Scratching the Beat Surface

Novels
The Mad Club
The Adept

Plays
The Mammals
The Beard
Gargoyle Cartoons
Gorf
Josephine: The Mouse Singer

Fragments of Perseus
Michael McClure

A NEW DIRECTIONS BOOK

ACKNOWLEDGMENTS
Grateful acknowledgment is given to the editors and publishers of magazines and books where some of the material in this volume previously appeared: *Arif Press Autumn List, Beat Angels, California Living, Co-Evolution Quarterly, Conjunctions, Credences, Ink, Journal for the Protection of All Beings, Kayak, New Wilderness Letter, Poetry Now, The Poetry Project Newsletter, Portland Review, Sparks of Fire, United Artists.* The poem "Fragments of Perseus" was first published as a book by Jordan Davies Press.

Manufactured in the United States of America
First published as New Directions Paperbook 554 in 1983
Published simultaneously in Canada by George J. McLeod, Ltd., Toronto

Library of Congress Cataloging in Publication Data

McClure, Michael.
  Fragments of Perseus.
  (A New Directions Book)
  I. Title.
PS3563.A262F7 1983   811'.54   83-2134
ISBN 0-8112-0867-2 (pbk.)

New Directions Books are published for James Laughlin
by New Directions Publishing Corporation
80 Eighth Avenue, New York, NY 10011

"Poetry is the language of a state of crisis."
—Stéphane Mallarmé

FRAGMENTS OF PERSEUS

1.

MEDUSA,

I
SEARCH

for you
in dreams
INSIDE OF DREAMS!

YOU ARE
the horror
of
my
mind

BLOWN
UP
with-

in

my body and MADE
INTO FLESH!

*
* *

MAKING
LOVE

TO
YOU

WAS LIKE
DRINKING

COLD WATER
running

NEAR
THE TOILETS.

It
had

a
taste.

* *
* *

I PLACE
the butchered
deer, wrapped
in his skin,

upon
the
floor.
He is my friend.

He is my brother
though
I
killed him.

2

He loves
the bronze-tipped
arrows.

Ice snaps from his pelt
and turns to water
on the stone floor.

*
* *

I SAW A LION
—a big one with a mane—
in the snow.
Also, two ravens.
An
eagle
soared over the cliffs
above the river

*
* *

THE IMAGE
OF
YOUR FACE
is out there

frozen in the ice
like a tiny sculpture

where the water melts
at the snowbank's base.

The wet snow that would be your hair

3

is in ripples

as moving snakes

would be.

IT
IS

BEAUTIFUL
and

it makes me ill. My stomach
clenches.

*
* *

((WHEN ZEUS
FELL UPON
MY MOTHER
in

a
shower
of gold

I was
conceived.

CAN
THAT
BE
TRUE?

4

How much of what I know
is real? How much is
imagining?))

* *
*

AND
YOU!

YOU!

YOU,
SNAKEHAIR!

* *
*

Imprisoned
in *not* remembering

my
muscles

be-

come

pained, perfect memory.

* *
*

A dead deer upon
the stone floor.
A lion playing
in the snow.

5

Life
is
a remembrance
of the inert

that's
taken

to

dancing.

Everything is all the same.

MEDUSA, THEY DO NOT SPEAK OF YOUR CHILDREN.
I tried not to look at them.
I
was
not
their father

and I did

not
want to be.
Like you, Snake Hair,
they

are
so
beautiful
they hurt the eyes.

You
knew
their
beauty
and you tried
to make me father them.

Those boys would go out and conquer
all the world for you

BUT
you'll
be
dead.

*
* *

I
TOLD

THEM
THAT

I
killed you.

Then I returned the power of invisibility . . . the cap
of blackness.

I took off the winged sandals.

I returned the game bag to the Stygian Nymphs
in their sensual grottoes.

—But,

I am turned to stone
because I did not say goodbye to you.

I
feel
my departure
eternally
because
it was not complete.

* *
*

I
hunt
deer
and
I ache.

*
* *

THE PROPHESY SAYS I WILL KILL MY GRANDFATHER.
I will not do that!

*
* *

Am I
caught between

deeds in the past
and actions in the future?

How much

if anything

is already sealed?

9

3.

MY MOTHER DANAE AND I
were sealed
in the ark, the casket,
by Grandpa

and hurled
in the river.

Downriver
Dektys
had
us

hauled out.
Dektys loved Mama but his brother
Polydektys

(I hated him)

de-
sired
her
most.

Polydektes tricked me.
He asked for a marriage gift
for his betrothal to Hippodameia.
I was so relieved that he'd leave Mama
alone
that I said I'd
bestow him anything.

Since I couldn't afford a horse for him
I said I'd even get the head of the Gorgonian
Medusa—if he wanted that.

He did!

*
* *

I'VE
ALWAYS
BEEN
CLOSE
TO
THE DEER—
always understood them.

I have

a different manner

of intelligence.

I suppose I'm easily tricked—and quick
to take revenge.

*
* *

ALSO, I'M INTENT
ON MY

honor.

*
* *

11

THE SWAN LADIES
had only one eye
and one tooth between
them.
They are in a very bright place
that alternately becomes
black for long
moments. They are out

on a cliff

but sometimes it is as if
they are also in a cave.

They are huge and laughable—harmless
idiotic.

I nearly felt guilty stealing their eye
from them. I grabbed it as they passed it
from one head to another.
They are big, smooth, shapeless,
birdy things—all wound
together—
blind heads and winglike flippers
going in and out of the central mass . . .

It

wasn't

at
all

what I expected.

Adventure is almost too easy.

*
* *

TO GET THEIR EYE

BACK

THEY TOLD ME

how to find
the Stygian Nymphs.
(HIDEOUS
BAGS
that
they
are
!)
Glamorous as their name sounds
those withered crones are as old
as volcanoes that bubbled up
in the world's beginning.
I'd rather fuck all the Swan Ladies
at once than smell the breath
of a Stygian Nymph
for the time it takes
a blue-bibbed lizard
to speed into his hole.
The Styx is the River of Hate
outside of Hell

but

the name

Rio Boredom

would fit more well.

"Zeus,"
I prayed, "Father Zeus,
give me the strength to tickle
all their jaded appetites."

I took

their drugs, went through
all the ceremonies. Sniffed all the gasses
rising from the marsh. Ate all the mushrooms

with them.

Still,
I couldn't stop seeing them
as they were. At last,
they gave me the black cap
that causes invisibility, the sandals
with the wings, and the game bag to hold
Medusa's head.

Away I sped.

*
* *

APPARENTLY
I

DREAM
ABOUT

these
things

over and over.
And they become dreams

inside of dreams
like you, Medusa.

*
* *

I

PUT

PIECES

of the deer

on spits and lean

them into the fire.

THE FIRE IS A MILLION

EYES OF MANY COLORS.

15

4.

ANDROMEDA,
I LOVE YOU.

I
LOVE

you the most.
You lie there sleeping

on the deerskins.
Your smile is beatific

like a girl child's.
Everything

that I
do, or am,

would have no
meaning

without your eyes
and smile.

THERE
ARE

      some things
      that go beyond
      our
      feelings.

WE

ARE
ONE

PERSON AND YET
I HAVE SECRETS FROM

YOU.

I do not control my destiny. I'm more free

than some

and yet I'm not
liberated.

*
* *

TO SLAY DRAGONS
to free you is

not
enough

when
I

am still chained

to my rock of self

above a howling sea.

*
* *

I CAN SEE HOW OUR MUSCLES BECOME RIGID
I feel how
I am not doing what I imagine

that I am.

I feel the body softly
crumple and make
a fold.
The fold is

re-enforced.

Soon,

we are other selves.

THE DEATH OF KIN CHUEN LOUIE

NOW, ON THE DAY BEFORE MY DAUGHTER'S
TWENTY-FIRST BIRTHDAY,
ON THE AFTERNOON OF HER PARTY,
I REVISIT THE SCENE OF THE DEATH
of Kin Chuen Louie.
He too was between twenty and twenty-one.
The newspapers called him
a smalltime extortionist.
But what are we all but small
time extortionists in the
proportionless
universe?
(I am in awe of the thought
of the coolness and sureness
of his assassin.)
Twelve days ago, on the Festival
of the Lord Buddha, shortly
after two in the afternoon,
Kin Chuen Louie left his flat
on Kearney Street.
Louie's young, long-haired murderer,
in black jacket and army pants,
waited with a .380
Walther automatic pistol holding
fourteen bullets. Kin Chuen Louie,
spotting his assailant, leaped
into his bright red Plymouth Fury.
The murderer stepped
to the driver's side and fired a shot
into Louie. Louie started the ignition
and slammed into reverse.

His foot stuck on the accelerator.
The car, propelled backward with great
force, jammed between
a building and a white car
parked there—knocking loose shards
of red brick painted over with beige.
The murderer stepped quickly
to the passenger side of the trapped
and roaring car and fired seven bullets
through the windshield
into a tight pattern on the head and neck
of Louie. A ninth shot missed,
going finger-deep
into brick. The killer
fled a few yards, turned at the corner,
and disappeared down Sonoma Alley.
A moment later,
we arrived on the empty street
and looked through
shattered glass
at the young Chinese man—
blood pouring out of the holes
in his head—slumped over
on his side. It was like the close-up
in a Sam Peckinpah movie.
He was completely relaxed
—finally and almost pleasantly limp
and serene—wearing an army jacket
and grubby levis . . . a slender, handsome,
clean-cut face with short hair boyishly
hanging in his eyes above
the dime-size bullet holes.
The blood pouring onto the seat covers
was a thick, reddish vermillion.

There was a peaceful, robbe-grilletish,
dim light inside the car.
The shattered window was like
a frosted spider web.
Either death is beautiful to see
—or we learn the esthetic
of death from films. BUT I do know
that our physical, athletic body,
a thing of perfect loops, and secret
and manifest
dimensions and breathings of consciousness
and unconsciousness, emanates
rainbows and actions,
and black flowers
and
it is there
to bear us through this world
and to kiss us goodbye at the doorstep
of any other.
I praise Everything-That-Is
for that blessing.
I drink chrysanthemum
tea in his memory.
Candied ginger, scented with licorice
from Hong Kong,
is on my breath.

I know each death

shall be as fine as his is.

BLUES

NOBODY CARES ABOUT YOUR FATHER!
No one cries about your mother!
They've gone to where
to old ghosts go.
They've burrowed themselves
in forgetful snow.
They've gone from sight
to where the dirt winds blow.
Ain't no way
to tell
what mole and earthworm
know.
BUT
still you
ache inside
where their living statues glow.
But still you ache inside where
their living statues glow.

CHANGER

for Russell

AT THE HOUR OF HIS BIRTH HE WAS
A WOLF-SHAPED CLOUD.
On his tenth breath he was a sea cave.
With the squirt of milk in his throat
he changed into a moon of Uranus.
When he first walked he was a butterfly landing
on a sailing ship.
Then
he was a pirate
and a sweating slave
at the oars. Soon
he was a sleek killer
whale.
Next
he became a buddha-like boulder
covered over
with mosses and nettles.
Next he was a shelf of fungus
on a cool tree trunk.
Then he became a giant elk
and a son of the wine god.
Next he became
a lake full of fish.
At last
he changed
into Proteus!

BEGINNING WITH LINES BY WHITEHEAD

for Dean Stockwell

IT IS THE BUSINESS OF THE FUTURE
TO BE DANGEROUS.
It is the love of the Divine
that inspires us!
It is the ecstasy
of lust
mixed with the play
of the mind
through perceptions
that changes
conceptions
to flashing colors
and soft gray and brown,
dream-like furs.

SONG

SURE, LET'S CELEBRATE THE BLACK SIDE
OF JOY. LET'S DROWN
the cup of cheer
in the barrel full of wine.
Let's see the wildflower's face,
all mauve and purple and bright yellow,
flattened by the pages
of a book—the spider
also pressed there
was once happy
chasing flies.

———————

I worship all that's black.
To be alive's a shock
like listening to an angel,
or a fairy,
singing in a rock.

BAJA BUNDLE

A DREAM IN THE TERRAZES MOTEL

"OH GOD," I CRIED, "SLAY ME,
hurt me, kill me!
Do anything but let
me go back to my beautiful house!"

There I was
a child again
in the museum
of my babyhood with
furniture stacked
around the walls
as in a warehouse.
And there on the blue
bureau—the enameled
blue bureau—was a sign
saying my parent's divorce
was an official one
of the normal kind.
THE HURT ROSE UP
and I could not
bear it.
"OH GOD," I CRIED, "SLAY ME,
hurt me, kill me!"
There was the perfect furniture
—the little wooden
highchair and the bas-
sinette—and I was
cut off from it then
by the divorce that
I never understood.
There was

NO WAY,
NO WAY
I would ever
go back to it!
And I woke up
forty-three years later
in the mid of the night
in Baja Mexico
under the skies
of frigate birds
and dark, ragged
golden eagles
and giant cacti—
and I write this down
for no one to read.

Mulege, Baja California

TO HENRY LUCE

After reading the Luce chapter of Halberstam's The Powers That Be
as excerpted in Esquire, *and remembering* Life *magazine's lies about the
Beat poets in 1959.*

THE POWERS THAT BE
ATTACKED US
with their tusks
in

blind fury

but

we have

left them

as empty husks
by our
persistance.

Still

their scale
entranced us

for a

decade.

We were saved
by the strength

of fears

and the tendons of

our tears.

THOUGHTS DURING FEVER
AT CABO SAN LUCAS

NOW WE HAVE JOINED THE WEALTHY.
(Dried orange wings of a butterfly,
with white dots on a border of black,
float over the desert
blowing this way and that.)
I lie with a chill
from the waves
of the Sea of Cortez.
Here we can smell the clouds
of scented wax from the machines
of the Indian workers
polishing the dark tiles,
and the molecular odors
of perfumed insecticides.
It
is
possible,
after the swimming,
that we
in the real
world
are totally free.
Here in the sunset.

ON A MOTORBOAT TRIP TO ISLA ESPIRITU SANCTU IN THE BAY OF LA PAZ, BAJA SUR

for the ghost of A. N. Whitehead

IT IS THE ADMISSION OF MORTALITY
THAT MAKES ME WHOLE.
I am my birth and death.
Each breath
takes me the longer
way toward the song
that's written on
the pale blue sky
by tails and wings
of frigate birds.
One day, I'll once again
become the soul
of the mountains and of stones.

FOR HARRY

I AM THE DEAD COYOTE ON THE ASPHALT
with my head turned back in glee.
I am the osprey nesting
on the road sign.
I am the eagle roosting
on the cactus tree.
I'm
whatever
the wind turns up to see.

BLACK PAPER SILHOUETTES
AT DISNEYLAND

HOW SAD ARE THE SILHOUETTES
that do not resemble us.

They show babes

with infant features

all clean cut

and in the burst of youth
like everyone imagines
self to be, before

opening their eyes

preceding mirror's truth.
How much happier
to be

the grizzled,

lovely,

laughing

survivors

that we are!

33

We're past the point
where Time can harm.

Disneyland—San Francisco

(END OF BAJA BUNDLE)

HYMN TO KWANNON

BEAUTIFUL KWANNON AND BEAUTEOUS GODDESSES
OF MERCY!
WE THANK YOU KWANNON.
WE THANK YOU GODDESSES OF MERCY.
HAVE PITY ON EVERYTHING.
HAVE PITY ON EVERYTHING.
HAVE PITY ON EVERYTHING.
BE KIND TO YOURSELF, AS ALLEN SAYS.
BRING GENTLENESS TO EVERY LIVING BODY.
HAVE PITY, HAVE MERCY.
EVERYTHING LIVES.
HAVE PITY—
MERCY.
MERCY—
PITY.
EVERYTHING LIVES.
BE KIND TO YOURSELF, AS ALLEN SAYS.
BRING JOY TO EYES THAT ARE STARS.
JOY TO EYES THAT
ARE STARS.
ERASE
OUR
PAINS.
WALK WITH SOFT HEALING FEET
OVER OUR GRIEFS.
EVERYTHING LIVES.
KWANNON AND GODDESSES OF MERCY
FROM EVERY SPACE
IN THE UNCARVED BLOCK,
HEALING BEINGS IN EVERY REALM,

COME AND STEAL OUR PAINS
AND LAUGH AND KISS THEM.
HAVE PITY, HAVE MERCY.
MERCY AND PITY.
BE KIND TO YOURSELVES.

COME KISS OUR GRIEFS
ON THEIR NOSES.
BE KIND TO THE BEASTS
CAUGHT IN THE TRAPS.
GIVE THEM GRAIN,
GIVE THEM SUGAR
AND FREEDOM.
MERCY FOR THOSE WHO LIE
IN THE MUD
OF
THE
WARS.
SAVE OUR BELOVED WHALES,
KWANNON,
KWANNON,
AND THOU,
OH GODDESSES OF MERCY.

WE CREATURES OF TURQUOISE AND FLESH AND
FLUFF,
OF TURQUOISE AND FLESH AND FLUFF.
CALL ON YOU.
EVERYTHING LIVES.
BEAUTIFUL KWANNON AND BEAUTEOUS GODDESSES
OF MERCY,
WE THANK YOU, WE THANK YOU.
KWANNON AND BEAUTEOUS GODDESSES OF MERCY!

GROGAN

GOODBYE EMMETT, GOODBYE
BEAUTIFUL FRIEND.
We all fly
into the end.

Your smile
is an eternal radiance.
Goodbye to the Diggers,
to subways,
and to dreams of mountain air.
You've beaten the snare

and kissed farewell
to the flesh.

You've slipped out of the net

and
pulled off

the clinging,
the clanging, mesh.

Goodbye,
farewell,

Emmett, beautiful friend.

SONG

I WORK WITH THE SHAPE
of spirit
moving the matter
in my hands;
I
mold
it from
the inner matrix.
Even a crow or fox
understands.

LISTEN LAWRENCE

LISTEN, LAWRENCE, THERE ARE CERTAIN OF US
INTENSELY COMMITTED
TO
a
real,
A REAL,
REVOLT! A REVOLT
that we only begin to
conceptualize as we
achieve it!
THE CONCEPTION
BEGINS SLOW
—as we do it—as we really do
it—as we make the revolution
with our bodies—our real BODIES!
OUR REAL BODIES ARE NOT DIVISIBLE
from the bulks of our
brother and sister beings!
We're alarmed by the simultaneous extinction
and overcrowding of creatures:
WE
BELIEVE
that the universe of discourse
(of talk and habit-patterned actions)
and the universe of politics
are equivalent!
THAT POLITICS IS DEAD
and
BIOLOGY
IS HERE!
We live near the shadow

AT THE NEAR EDGE OF THE SHADOW
                              ((TOO NEAR!!))
              of the extermination
              of the diversity
              of living beings. No need
              to list their names
        (Mountain Gorilla, Grizzly, Dune Tansy)
                    for it
              is a too terrible
              elegy to do so!

              COMMUNISM,
              CAPITALISM,
              SOCIALISM,
                will do
              NOTHING,
              NOTHING
              to save the surge
        of life—the ten thousand
        to the ten-thousandth, vast,
        Da Vincian molecule of which
              ALL LIFE,
              ALL LIFE
              is a particle!

                    *

        LISTEN, BELIEVE
                    ME,
        none of us can afford to luxuriate,
        if we care about the presence of life.
                    The
                whole scene
        IS ALL ONE DIMENSIONAL!
              MARCUSE was right!

                    40

because he saw there is
only one, one-dimensional, planet-wide civilization
and realpolitik.
Unfortunately
it is modelled on one of the most
perfect aspects of our nature: THE DESIRE
TO GROW, TO WASTE, TO BREED, TO BURN UP,
TO EAT, TO TOSS DOWN, TO TEAR UP, TO FINGER
AND TWIST, AND TEASE, AND MAKE ALL
THINGS TERRIBLE AND DIVINE,
AND GLORIOUS! And we have
succeeded TOO WELL,
TOO WELL!
We are the most complete successes
the world has ever known!
POLITICS
is
part
and particle
of this horrific success, success
which is—in fact—an explosion that has
ALREADY OCCURRED. We have charred
the surface of the earth leaving behind
buildings which are cinders from the blasts
of oceans of petrochemicals!
Look, books and papers are
the fossil fuel explosion of trees!
LISTEN, LAWRENCE, this
is the same old politics! ANY, ANY, ANY
POLITICS
is the POLITICS OF EXTINCTION!

*

IT IS TIME FOR PEOPLE TO COME OUT OF THE CLOSET
ALL RIGHT,
ALL RIGHT!
IT IS TIME FOR THEM
to come out of the closet—
OUT OF THE CLOSET OF POLITICS
and into the light of their flesh and bodies!
NOW
is
THE TIME
to learn to see
with the systemless system
—with the systemless system
like a Negative Capability—
of anarchist-mammal perception!
THAT'S BIOLOGY! Now is the time
to see that
it is our nature to be beautiful
and the destruction wrought by politics
is part of our beauty. Now we can learn
to see why it is our nature to go on with
this destructive politics. NOW WE CAN SAY:
LET'S STOP! LET'S STOP
THIS ENDLESS MURDER BY POLITICS!
LET
US
DO WHAT
WE CAN TO STOP
so very much useless pain!

It is our nature to overbreed and to kill!
But our nature has endless dimensions! We
can choose among them—we can reject,
we can reject the flowers of politics!

42

MEMORIES FROM CHILDHOOD

I REMEMBER THE FIELDS
of Kansas and the laws

that made
them flat and bare

I know when and where
the field mouse died.

I watched the rivers tried
for treason,

then laid straight,
and the cottonwood and opossum

placed upon the grate
of petroleum civilization!

I
go

back, in my mind,
to where I came from!

"IT'S NATION TIME"

NOW IT IS TIME FOR A NATION,
FOR A SPIRITUAL
NATION,
a spiritual Nation
based
and formed on open freedom,
on flesh and biology—on what we can know
of the shaping
of men and all living creatures
as we grow together
through billions of years! And
IT
MUST
INCORPORATE
(hold in the body of the Nation)
our ceaseless need
for liberation, for revolt,
and for CHANGE!

WATCHING THE STOLEN ROSE

THE ROSE IS A PINK-YELLOW
UNIVERSE UNFOLDING

layer upon
luminous layer

petal to petal
spreading

unsteady yet
perfectly balanced

as the curling
of smoke

from a mind
on fire.

LITTLE ODE

for Joanna

AND DEATH SHALL HAVE NO TERROR WHEN LOVE
MAY BALANCE THEE, MADONNA, IN MY HEART.
I shall die with the wrinkled lines
around thy eyes upon my shield
of consciousness.
I confess
I worship thee
and all material things.

Rose petals falling!

The secret loves of wolves!

Deer mice trembling in the snow!

Turquoise set in worn and darkened silver!

46

ACTION PHILOSOPHY

THAT GOVERNMENT IS BEST WHICH GOVERNS LEAST.
Let me be free of ligaments and tendencies
to change myself into a shape
that's less than spirit.
LET ME BE A WOLF,
a caterpillar, a salmon,
or
an
OTTER
sailing in the silver water
beneath the rosy sky.
Were I a moth or condor
you'd see me fly!
I love this meat of which I'm made!
I dive in it to find the simplest vital shape!

AH! HERE'S THE CHILD!!!

*WHAT'S LIBERTY WHEN ONE CLASS STARVES
ANOTHER?*

ON THE AVENUE—FIFTH AVENUE

OH. AH. CHILDHOOD RAGES IN THE FIRE!
Wolf-flames of Past are a solid Block
we dance upon.
Sirens howl through orange
falling leaves.
Horses munch grass
among gas fumes.
Like you, I wonder
where
we've gone!
Note,
the moth holes in our capes
of immortality. See,
our flesh is permanent!
We'll hold hands
like living statues
in the future falling snow!

LEAVING THE REHEARSAL: N.Y.C.

THE SMELL OF MADNESS! FUMES
and smoke and rubber tires
and mint gum and broken bodies
—BROKEN BODIES—
flashing
in the glint of subway glare.

I'm happy as a babe
—a man within
it all: urine, shit, sweat,
mumbled speech, fumbled clutch
at nothingness
and falling, spinning, yellow leaves.

BLACK WORDS

KEEP THE LAWS OFF MY BODY!
I breathe the musky
odor of cowardice
but I am a man;
my courage is growing.

.

I am writing a revolution
BUT MY BONES ARE FUCHSIAS.
I need strength to love
but I am a midget
of spirit.

SEE, MY WOLF THOUGHTS!

ME-OH

SURE! LET ME BURST AGAIN AND SEE WHO I AM—
IN THIS BLACKNESS SEEKING
MIDDLE AGE! WHO AM I BY THIS STAR
on this whirling ball where I can sense
a billion galaxies in clusters
and smell the lucid light around the city's
towers while the sky dies in rosy layers
and I remember all the soft soft feet
and toes that crept across
my childish life that stands
as sizeless as the daydreams
of a virus. I am a pouring
flowing crystal. I'm the midnight
voices of the mating swallows!
I'm the tow truck of the soul
that I create around me

AS

I

CROSS THIS BLAZING BRIDGE!

I AM THE WOLF, THE HUMMINGBIRD,

THE BOYCHILD

IN THE GRAYBEARD MAN!

CAPTIVES

WHAT A PIECE OF BLACK
SPIRIT YOU ARE,

you who come
through the door

with a sleek
long tail

and yellow eyes
to sit

on my knees
as I hold

you against
your will

and I get giddy
feeling your captive

body as the harp-
sichord plays Bach.

VAN DYKE

WE HAVE THIS QUALITY
OF OTHERNESS,
this majesty

that shows
from corners

of the eye
and smiles

—like black stars
on an orange sky,

like eagle claws
upon a chickadee.

DREAM: THE NIGHT OF DECEMBER 23RD

For Jane

—ALL HUGE LIKE GIANT FLIGHTLESS KIWIS TWICE
THE SIZE OF OSTRICHES,
they turned and walked away from us
and you were there Jane and you were twenty-two
but this was the nineteen-forties,
in Wichita, near the edge of town, in a field
surrounded by a copse of cottonwoods. It was
getting dark and the trees around the bridge
almost glowed like a scene by Palmer.
The two Giant Birds—Aepyorni—from Madagascar,
extincted A.D. one thousand, turned and walked
from us across the bridge. Even in the semi-darkness
the softness of their brown feathers made
curls pliant as a young mother's hair. There
was a sweet submission in the power of their enormous
legs (giant drumsticks). Their tiny heads
(in proportion to their bodies) were bent
utterly submerged in their business and sweeping
side to side as a salmon does—or as a wolf does—
but with a Pleistocene, self-involved gentleness
beyond our ken. My heart rose in my chest
(as the metaphysical poets say "with
purple wings of joy.") to see them back
in life again. We both looked, holding hands,
and I felt your wide-eyed drinking-in

of things.
Then I turned and viewed across the darkening

field and there was a huge flightless hunting fowl
(the kind that ate mammals in the Pliocene).
He stood on one leg in the setting sun by the sparkling
stream that cut across the meadow to the bridge.
He had a hammer head and curled beak, and after my
initial surge of fear to see the field was dotted,
populated, by his brethren, each standing in the setting

sun, I saw their stately nobility

and again

the self-involvement.

We followed the Aepyorni

across the old wooden bridge made of huge
timbers. The bridge was dark from the shadows
of the poplars and the evergreens there.
The stream was dimpled with flashing moonlight

—and I think it had a little song.

Then

I found that on the bridge we were among
a herd of black Wildebeests—Black Gnus.
One was two feet away—turned toward me—
looking me eye-into-eye. There was primal
wildness in the upstanding coarse (not
sleek as it really is in Africa) fur on
the knobby, powerful-like-buffalo shoulders.
(Remember this is a dream.) I passed by him
both afraid and unafraid of wildness as I had passed

through the herd of zebras at the top of Ngorongoro Crater
in front of the lodge, where from the cliff we could see
a herd of elephants like ants, and the soda lake
looked pink because of flamingos there.
There is an essence in fear overcome
and I overcame fright in passing by those zebras

and this black Wildebeest.

Then we passed

over the heavy bridge and down a little trail
on the far side of the meadow, walking back

in the direction we had been.

Soon we came

to a cottage of white clapboards
behind a big white clapboard house and knocked
on the door; it was answered by a young man
with long hair who was from the Incredible String Band.
He took us inside and he played an instrument
like a guitar and he danced as he played it.
The lyre-guitar was covered with square plastic
buttons in rows of given sizes and shapes.
The instrument would make any sound, play
any blues, make any creature sound, play
any melody . . . I wanted it
badly—it was a joy. My chest rose.
I figured I'd have to, and would be glad to,
give twenty or thirty thousand for it . . .
Then the dream broke
and I was standing somewhere with Joanna

to the side of a crowd of people by a wall
of masonry and I reached into my mouth
and took from my jaw (all the other
persons vanished and I was the center of everything)
a piece which was eight teeth
fused together. I stared at them
wondering how they could all be one piece.
They were white . . . It was some new fossil.
Down on the bone there were indentations like rivulets
like the flowing pattern of little rivers.

INSIDE THIS HILL

*(A dream following John Wasserman's mortal accident—a remembrance
of the scene of the accident—and a return to the dream.)*

AND THERE WAS JOHN, TALL JOHN, WALKING, ACROSS
                                    THE GREENSWARD
of a campus—perhaps Kent State or Yale. He did not know
that he was dead, that he had died three weeks before
          in a head-on car crash or that we
had seen the wreck on our way to view a film he
recommended in his column. We drove slowly
peering through the rain at the car overturned
in roadside blackness where it blazed orange-red
          like a giant flaming match head.
Returning twenty minutes later from the sold-out
theater we saw the car again—John's car—beside the cinder
of the burned hulk. The front end had been pushed
concave and was in the front seat. I was stilled
by the thought of death there, and the quickness
of mortality—not knowing it was John. In the morning
          Jane told me John had died on 280.

Now I have dreamed of John striding along a campus.

          In the night, I ran after John shouting
          but he did not hear. Then I remembered
the dead can return for a while to complete unfinished
business—but they do not know they are dead.
John was preoccupied—in his hand he held
a pad of paper—and he walked with mouth
half open, smiling to himself, looking young
and affable, and handsome in his gray hair
and black tee-shirt. I knew I must not tell John
that he was dead. He looked so abstracted, caught

58

in his business, and almost happy. I spoke
to him. I put my arm around his shoulder
but that embarrassed him. He pushed me away,
and walked on and I began to cry to see him dead.

It is March on Twin Peaks where I stop to write
this—there are new flowers—mauve mallow,
purple lupine, sorrel, buttercups, and golden
tracks of spring as if some joyous bear had walked here
with flowered feet and scattered prints
behind—and John is still here
in the generous beauty of his presence—but also
he is inside this hill where all spring flowers are black:
black mallow, black lupine, black sorrel,
black buttercups and black tracks of spring.

TWO SPEEDS

for Jane

1.

THE DEER
leaps
at
us
nearly
striking
the
moving
car
in
the
darkness.

2.

THE BRONZE-GREEN
HUMMINGBIRD HURLS
himself upward
like a pellet
from the sling
of his own brain.
He chases the scarlet
blur of the tee-shirt
as it sails
through the air.

Then,
eye-to-eye with
the sun-bathing girl
on the roof,
he
hovers in front of her
just as she catches
the tee-shirt.

LARGO FOR THE MONSTER

WE ARE BUT WAVES OF LIGHT CONSTRAINED BY WALLS
OF CIRCUMSTANCE,
WE ARE BUT WAVES OF LIGHT CONSTRAINED BY WALLS
OF CIRCUMSTANCE,
WE ARE BUT WAVES OF LIGHT CONSTRAINED BY WALLS
OF CIRCUMSTANCE,
WE ARE DEAD HORSES IN A PIT, WE ARE DEAD
HORSES IN A PIT,
WE ARE DEAD HORSES IN A PIT THAT LIE AND
MOULDER
WITH OUR BODY'S FUR ON BODY'S FUR AND OUR
VOICES
FROZEN,
FROZEN IN ETERNITY!

WE ARE RED BITES OF APPLE SKIN
WITHIN THE MOUTH, WE ARE RED BITES
OF APPLE SKIN WITHIN THE MOUTH.
WE ARE THE YELLOW PANSY IN THE WINDY FIELD!
We are the yellow pansy in the windy field!
We are the consciousness that bounds

WE ARE THE CONSCIOUSNESS THAT BOUNDS
WE ARE THE CONSCIOUSNESS THAT BOUNDS

that bounds and leaps,
the consciousness that bounds and leaps

and laughs within the boy who weeps
upon the bed. He holds his head
and screams.
He holds his head and screams.

WE ARE DEAD HORSES IN A PIT

                constrained by walls
                constrained by walls
                constrained by walls
                        of
                circumstance.

        WE ARE THE ODES TO SILENCE
            we are the odes to silence
                    that

            OUR
            SELVES
            contain.
WE ARE THE FAME WE EAT WITH SALT AND BITTER
                            OIL!
    WE ARE THE ENDLESS TOIL THAT SEEKS
            TO GROW WITHIN
            THE ROTTED CREAM
            within the curdled cream
            of longing emptiness.

        He sees his father drunk and gone
        constrained by walls of circumstance,

                HIS
            MOTHER, DRINKING

        LAUGHING AT THE DANCE—
    Maid of Light entranced by floors of circumstance.

    His ears that burst with shock and horror scream.
HIS EYES BLOT OUT THE SHEEN, HIS EYES BLOT
                    OUT THE SHEEN

                        63

of visions there
of visions there

and present the hare that's nuzzling
in the grass. The Mass
of all things happening
IS LOST

AND

HE DIES.

HE DIES AND RISES,

RISES, SPLASHING, AND HE SPREADS
in the sea of otters, into

A MICKEY MOUSE, A DUCK,

A THOUSAND CLOWNS,
A THOUSAND CLOWNS.

˙Oh, yeah, he's bitter
AND HE HATES. HE HATES

all men and women and he makes shapes
and he makes shapes constrained by walls
of circumstance:
A MICKEY MOUSE, A DUCK,
a thousand clowns,
a Porky Pig, a Goofy Hound,
Dopey, Doc—and Bugs.
He's the Three Little Pigs
confronted by the Big Bad Wolf.

The gulf,
THE
PIT,
feeds back
the fantasy
that he's a horse, a mule,
a bulk, a beast that's dying in
a pit.
Then he's dead again, but builds
himself into the system of his boats
made out of spools and twine
and boards from apple boxes.
Foxes
speaking of sour grapes
are not more eloquent than he.

I
CANNOT STAND THE PAIN!
I CANNOT STAND THE PAIN

that makes me silent, absent
as an elf. It's caught
within the self
and ever faces me.
I am the pain I always see

I am the pain I always see
and never know.

It

IS

THE ABSENCE OF A FATHER'S SMILE,

of the sculptured act
to emulate
(that I may be
the father of my acts).

IT'S THE SHAKING INSECURITY OF WHO I AM.
I am not a yellow pansy in a windswept field.
I am not waves of light constrained.

Sometimes I am the things I yield
to fears I cannot see.

COULD

I

BUT

LOOK BACKWARD THROUGH MY TEARS!!!!

And there I am all fat and soft and amiable,
tearful, a sweaty cherub,
locked in lying still, all filled
with hopes the images will pass.
LET ME BE FREE OF THIS AWFUL THING!
I am but waves of light constrained by walls of circumstance.
I'M
anything
but what
I am:
I'm a snoozling mouse, or Henny Penny,
or rodents walking through the snow
to hollow logs; I'm hungry shrews,

66

and coons—like Ibiddy, like Bibiddy,
like Sibiddy, like Sap, like Nibs.
When I hurt I'm turtles without shells. I'm peeled
like
tangerines.
I'm drowning in the rivers of my tears.

I'M A HEAP OF LEAVES RAKED INTO A HOLE
OF GRIEF!

I'M A HEAP OF LEAVES
I'M A HEAP OF LEAVES
I'M A HEAP OF LEAVES
I'M A HEAP OF LEAVES

RAKED INTO A HOLE
RAKED INTO A HOLE
RAKED INTO A HOLE

I'M A HEAP OF LEAVES
RAKED INTO A HOLE
OF GRIEF.

I'M A HEAP OF LEAVES
RAKED INTO A HOLE
OF GRIEF.

FLOW THROUGH THE SYSTEM

for Harold and Lu Morowitz

LET ENERGY FLOW THROUGH THE SYSTEM
TO EXPERIENCE THE SYSTEM:
the billows and roils and harsh spots
are not plots
but nodes and spurs that can drive desire
to create new shapes. The moths
of what-we-know upon the window ledge
are also condors
soaring over hills.

What

WE

BUILD

is made from tiny things
like crumpled molecules of oil
and meat that hold a thousand systems
in each bite or drop!

BUFFALO MOTEL

for Bill King

—WATCH GENET ON T.V.
in color.
The Maids prance.

Systems
dance.

This
is
decadence.

This is really it
and sweet Saint Jean
is proto-punk

with gold and ivory
tongue.

ON AN IMAGINARY ETCHING
BY SAMUEL PALMER

BLACK SHEEP MOVE THROUGH
                        THE DEEP
            SNOW;
        the turquoise glow
                of strange sparks
            on the cold flint
            is hidden from
                    the bearded men
                by the glint
                        of the day
            dropping into
                the night.
        The new moon
                rises
            over the tower.
        The nocturnal heron
        dreams of his flight.
            Frogs are still
                in the ice.

DREAM: NIGHT OF MARCH 5TH

WE ARE ALL IN THE SOUP TOGETHER! NO!
It is not soup! It is brown gravy and steaming
hot—not enough to burn—but warm as it was
on those roast beef sandwiches.—And there
are kids in this vat of brown gravy with me.
They are children but truly they're small, grown men
and women. Beautiful women with blonde
hair but kids. Good looking young men
but children. They are small people. They sit
in the brown gravy up to their chins. They speak
to one another and they look at me. I don't
recognize any of them. I must swim
to the other side of the vat and do not want
to—I must lower my head under the surface.
I begin—and I stop.
It is revolting but I must do it. It clings.
We are high on a platform in the great tub
and the ceiling is close but I can't see it
for the thickness of the steam prevents
that—BUT I know the roof is nacre, is mother-
of-pearl, and is filled with niches
like a vision—like separate visions—
with a drama in each one of them.
BUT
EACH
ONE
IS
not what I expected.
Oh, see! Spidery men in blue costumes!
Ray guns! Hurricanes. Beaches with sun

and palm trees! Swords and pools of blood
filled with roses. Chinchillas eating
shamrocks under dark mysterious tables
where old folks above drink from cut
glass and wipe their lips
on lacy napery.
Go crazy
bite their legs
and boots!

.

Commit yourself! Engage!
It is beautiful!

DREAM: NIGHT OF MARCH 7TH

THE SMALL WHITE DOG BARKS ON THE ROUGH HILLSIDE

that is Tank Hill—here above my house.
He shakes up the passers-by on the sidewalk
below. He's like a Samoyed but a bit
smaller. He's perky and bright and de-
fiant. When we run up from the street
he goes round the hill and we chase him.
He cuts down the slope into the rough land
below where there is gray granite in outbreaks,
and some scrub, and we throw rocks at him.
We realize we'll hurt people by throwing
stones. We'll have to catch him
and stop him or kill him. People go wild
chasing him and I run along easily beside them.
As they pursue there is a pack instinct
that is growing. More people join the crowd
that is chasing the white dog. He scurries
along ahead of us—over rough draws
and always up hillsides. It is like a lynch mob
or a pack after a deer, and the feeling
gets me. My chest grows, swells with good
feeling. My heart beats. IT'S THRILLING!
Now I'm part of the troop chasing the white
mutt (which, in fact, is like the mouse Jerry
in the *Tom & Jerry* cartoon when he is
wearing the foxy dog head). Now
I'm one of them—the mob. We've
trapped the defiant white dog. He's
in a cul de sac above us. Now he's
turned around and he's scampering towards us
hoping to break our line. He can't

do it. *Hey*, I think, *he's got the spirit*
of Coyote. We need him! I put
on an extra surge of speed and rush
up the hill past the yelling mob. I bend
down without stopping and grab the dog,
tucking him under my arm, and I swing back
in a turn, and burst through the crowd
climbing up after us. . .

I'm crazy about
this dog. And we're one!
HE'S PART OF ME!
I

L
O
V
E

HIM
!

POEM BY AMIRI BARAKA

Poem by Amiri Baraka was written at the autumn equinox. I was sleeping under the stars on the house deck and dreamed I was typing a poem by Baraka. The poem had a spirit shape and on awakening I held it in my mind's eye and typed it. The column of sounds is part of the poem.

	A man
	is what
Balang	he is and always
	must be. You see there is Death
AG	in the wings. The wings of Death hover
	over me. There's now now
AG	No Way—No Way to call it back
Boro	or re-create the dead hands to hold
	me or thee. We glow like the breeze
NAHG	on the pink or black skin. The win
	is too late to conquer the ease with
AH	which we enter the dark. The lark
TH	on the fences hangs there in CHILD
	HOOD like Robin and Little John and Maid
N–NN	Marian.

Call us back to cities.
Call us back to the SLEAZE. Note
I am not you. This is not what you wrote.
The old men are young now on the street
below. They're kids with their bottles
planning a joke.
This is your stroke and not mine.
Wine turns them on. Young and tanned
with beards and big bellies like Odysseus
rising, trapped in vino, from Homer.

Franz Kline
dead drunk and joyously talking at the Cedar.

It's all part of the great
brush that we have with the law.
We gnaw ourselves sick with it.
But still we are here with dark on
                           our wings.
    The lady calling her cat wakes me
at dawn. She's down facing the lawn
from her back porch. Making baby
calls to the puss. I know,
I know she's the universe's center.

                        Any point is
                        the center
                            of things.
                    The starling squawking
                or the kids on boats
                    starving in Asia.
                I listen to the voices
        of honored mass murderers on the old radio/
of honored mass murderers on the old radio

WITH A LINE BY ROBERT HERRICK

OSPREY   DUST

LIFE IS THE BODY'S LIGHT
but you don't know
WHAT LOVING'S ALL ABOUT.
Sea Urchin recognizes
self in a pool and she
can SHOUT!
M
E
A
T
CROSSES
blaze
in
THE NIGHT!

—All we are is skin

and FLIGHT

SILVER   MOTH

MOTH   SILVER

OSPREY   MOTH

SILVER   DUST

DUST OSPREY

SILVER

MOTH

STANZAS COMPOSED IN TURMOIL

The motile spirochete-like organism became more and more intimately associated with its aerobic mitochondria-containing amoeboid host.
—*Lynn Margulis*, Origin of Eukaryotic Cells

AND SO THE PARTS OF ME ARE DRAWN TOGETHER
BACK ALL THOSE BILLION YEARS, 3000
million years—No! Still more!
AND
FURTHER

back
and
BACK!

I am a cell!
I'm a cell within
a cell!

I'M
something
else.

I'm the Beatles.
I'm a MAMMAL
moving

BUT

WAY WAY WAY WAY WAY WAY WAY WAY

back
there

I'm part of you
as we explode out
of that black ball

into these realms
of fantasy! Hear
me tell you there

are fuchsias here upon
the table in that vase
upon the tartan, mohair drape

of blue, green, white, red.
—*And listen* to the sirens whooping
in the morning air!

SURE

THAT'S

THE WAY IT IS! IT'S NATION

TIME!

Time to wake up!
We are the Nations of our selves
drawn together. WE ARE IN DANGER

OF THE LOSS OF OUR DEEP

((OUR DEEP DEEP)) BEHAVIOR

IN THESE AWFUL CRUELTIES TO WHICH
we've brought (and created with)
our appetitions!

NOTHING MATTERS BUT MY LIBERTY!

WITHOUT MY LIBERTY, YOU'RE NOTHING, *NADA*,

ZERO!

(WHEN THOSE PARTS OF ME PULLED TOGETHER
THEY GAVE ME MOTILITY)
WHEN THE MITOCHONDRIA-BEING (Respirator) pulled into
his/hers/its protector
it found the universe and was joined by

a brother/sister organelle—the tail
(whip-mover—whip for all things are pain
and movement in this . . .)   THIS . . .)

LET'S GO! LET'S MOVE! ALL
IS BEAUTY; all is motion; let's move
ourselves within ourselves. KEEP IT

A–
LIVE!
YOU'RE GORGEOUS!

•
•
•

Your lovely soft brown skin I suck down my
gorge. Whether withered or maybe new. All
these years I do it. Time becomes real as
it becomes us. But you can drop it. DROP
IT!
DROP
IT!
WE'RE FREE! We're lib-
erated. We used our guilt to sharpen
senses. I can sight, sound, taste, touch, smell,
or gorge on you. Forge you into what you are as
you free me with your chains. Change is
what we're up to.—Why
I'm almost as mad about you as
YOU

ARE

ABOUT

ME
!

We're gold ostriches
running on the veldt of Time
looking for a place to stick our heads
while we flap our plumey wings.
WE'RE BACTERIA STUCK TOGETHER SINGING
(one-inside-the-other)
making motion.

PULSING / STREAMING

WHY, I CAN TELL YOU WE DON'T EXIST.
WAR, LOVE, REVOLUTION, DO NOT HELP
A BIT!

WE'RE THE LOST IMAGININGS OF INDRA'S NET
MELTED IN THE SOLID PULP OF NOTHING STUFF.

WE KNOW WHAT WE'RE DOING! LEONARDO DOESN'T
DO IT BETTER. THIS IS THE WAY IT ALWAYS IS
AND WAS. The Big Dipper
setting on the horizon edge
is our cup. We wake in the night
to look out on black cliffs in gray
fog. We've kissed each other ten
thousand times, nude upon the beach
after bathing in the icy waves
in mud-blue water while the kelp
is dragging at our legs.
                    The parts
            of us joined
            TOGETHER
        long ago to bring
        us to this place where
    LOVE is the only answer
            that

            we've
            got.

It doesn't help a bit.
It thrills and pains
as bad as ever.
STILL,
you free me,
you move me, you're
my motility, my freedom.
I'M
YOURS. It's
a mystery. It's hypostatized.

BREATH
HELPS

and your wrinkled smile,
and your toes running on the black
stones where the foam hits.

WE'RE BARELY HERE AND IT WAVERS, QUAVERS,
THRILLS, chills
me till I could scream and
fall apart again.

BUT WAY WAY WAY WAY

WAY WAY

WAY DOWN DEEP INSIDE
my core and yours
/which is everywhere and nowhere/

83

WE'RE

IN

DANGER

OF THE LOSS OF OUR DEEP

((OUR DEEP DEEP)) BEHAVIOR!

WE'RE ALWAYS THERE, ALWAYS AT
AN EDGE, ALWAYS TIP-TOEING
ON THE CRACK OF CRISIS.
OUR PHYSIOLOGY IS THE STATE OF CRISIS.

THE AWFUL
CRUELTIES

are us.
Are in-

distinguishable
from joys. Our sharing

eats our mammal brothers,
devours crustacean sisters

mating in the tide. WE BURN

INSIDE!
The white-tailed kite

hovers in the warming sun.
He looks for

the meadow mouse
with a silver star reflected in his eyes.

LET'S LOVE THE CRUELTIES

WE CRUELLY STOP

till we burst into self-consuming flames creating
us. HEY, we're in the car roar.
We're in the car roar. We're in the car roar.
Hey, we're in the car roar. We're in the car roar.
HEY!   HEY   HEY   HEY   HEY   HEY!

WE'RE   WE'RE

IN   IN

DANGER   DANGER

OF THE LOSS OF OUR DEEP, OUR DEEP BEHAVIOR.

I AM MY DEEP BEHAVIOR!

I'M MY DEEP BEHAVIOR!

I'M MY DEEP BEHAVIOR!

Dancing in my hungers!
Dancing in my hungers!

I AM ME-THOU-THEE! ME-THOU-THEE!

WE ARE THE NATION! WE ARE THE NATION!

WE ARE THE NATION! WE ARE THE NATION!

IN THE GLORY OF THE ACID RAIN WE ARE THE NATION!
In the rising buildings—Mammal Nation!
In the crumbling light we are the Nation!
WHAT WE ARE

INSIDE,

BELOW THE SOCIAL WHIRLING,

IS THE NATION, NATION, NATION,

IS THE NATION, MAMMAL NATION!

We're in danger.

THAT'S WHAT WE LOVE!

WE LOVE THIS DANGER!

WE ARE DEEP INSIDE!
WE ARE DEEP INSIDE!
WE ARE DEEP INSIDE!
WE ARE DEEP INSIDE!

WE ARE DEEP INSIDE!
WE ARE DEEP INSIDE!
WE ARE DEEP INSIDE!
WE ARE DEEP INSIDE!
WE ARE DEEP INSIDE
dancing in the car roar,
dancing on the beaches in the car roar,
dancing on the beaches in the car roar
in the Acid Rain, in the Acid Rain. No fear!
NO FEAR! NO FEAR! HEY! NO FEAR! NO FEAR! HEY!
NO FEAR!

San Francisco, Mendocino

INDEX
OF TITLES
AND FIRST LINES

89